Ladybird  Readers

# Daddy Pig's Office

# Series Editor: Sorrel Pitts
# Text adapted by Sorrel Pitts

LADYBIRD BOOKS

UK | USA | Canada | Ireland | Australia
India | New Zealand | South Africa

Ladybird Books is part of the Penguin Random House group of companies
whose addresses can be found at global.penguinrandomhouse.com.
www.penguin.co.uk    www.puffin.co.uk    www.ladybird.co.uk

Penguin
Random House
UK

Text adapted from *Peppa Pig: Daddy Pig's Office*, first published by Ladybird Books, 2008
This version first published by Ladybird Books, 2017
001

This book copyright © ABD Ltd/Ent. One UK Ltd 2017

This book is based on the
TV Series 'Peppa Pig'.
'Peppa Pig' is created by
Neville Astley and Mark Baker.
Peppa Pig © Astley Baker Davies Ltd/
Entertainment One UK Ltd 2003.

www.peppapig.com

Printed in China

A CIP catalogue record for this book is available from the British Library

ISBN: 978–0–241–29814–5

All correspondence to:
Ladybird Books
Penguin Random House Children's
80 Strand, London WC2R 0RL

MIX
Paper from
responsible sources
FSC® C018179

# Daddy Pig's Office

Based on the Peppa Pig
TV series

# Picture words

Peppa

Daddy Pig

George

Mrs Cat

Mr Rabbit

computer

printer

office

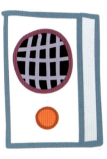

buzzer

elevator

stamp

Peppa and George
wanted to see
Daddy Pig's office.

"What do you do
at your office?"
asked Peppa.

"I can show you!"
said Daddy Pig.

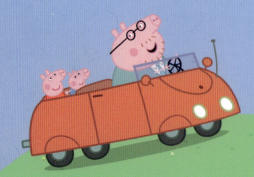

"This is the buzzer," said Daddy Pig.

"Can I put my finger on the button?" asked Peppa.

"Yes," said Daddy Pig.

Peppa put her finger on the button. "Hello?" said Peppa.

Then, the door opened.

9

"This is the elevator,"
said Daddy Pig.

"Can I put my finger
on the button?"
asked Peppa.

"No, George can put his finger on it," said Daddy Pig.

George put his finger on the elevator button.

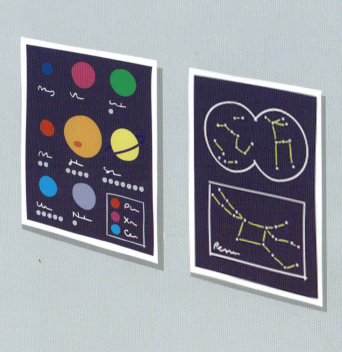

The elevator went up
to Daddy Pig's office.

Daddy Pig, Peppa,
and George all went
into the office.

"This is Mrs Cat," said Daddy Pig.

"Hello, Mrs Cat," said Peppa.

"This is Mr Rabbit,"
said Daddy Pig.

"Hello, Mr Rabbit,"
said Peppa.

"I'm showing Peppa and George my office," said Daddy Pig.

"I do this at my desk,"
said Mr Rabbit.

He put a stamp on some paper.

"Can I do that?" asked Peppa.

"Yes," said Mr Rabbit.

Peppa put lots of stamps
on some paper.

Stamp, stamp, stamp!

IN

"I've got a computer and a printer on my desk," said Mrs Cat.

She drew a picture on
her computer.

"Can I do that?" asked Peppa.

"No, George can do it now," said Daddy Pig.

George drew a picture on the computer.

George and Peppa printed
with Mrs Cat's printer.

Print, print, print!

"What a lot of paper!"
said Mrs Cat.

"Let's go to my desk,"
said Daddy Pig.

"Do you have a stamp and a computer?" asked Peppa.

"No," said Daddy Pig.
"But I have pens!"

"Pens are good! Can we draw with your pens?" asked Peppa.

Peppa and George liked
Daddy Pig's pens.

"I like drawing in your
office!" said Peppa.

Draw, draw, draw!

"Let's go home now,"
said Daddy Pig.

Daddy Pig's office was fun.

"I like Mr Rabbit's job, and I like Mrs Cat's job, but I like your job too, Daddy!" said Peppa.

# Activities

The key below describes the skills practiced in each activity.

🖊️ Spelling and writing

📖 Reading

💬 Speaking

❓ Critical thinking

✴️ Preparation for the Cambridge Young Learners Exams

**1** Match the words to the pictures.

1  Mrs Cat

2  Peppa

3  Daddy Pig

4  Mr Rabbit

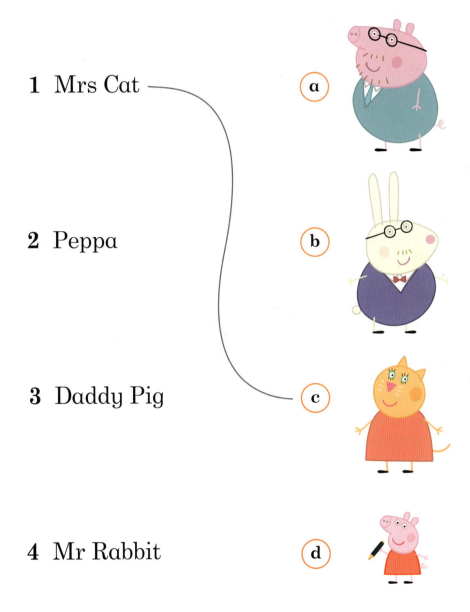

a

b

c

d

## 2 Look at the pictures. Write the correct words on the lines.

office    buzzer    elevator    stamp

**1**

elevator

**2**

_____

**3**

_____

**4**

_____

**3** Write *Peppa, George,* or *Daddy Pig.* 📖 🖊

1        <u>Peppa</u>      and George wanted to see Daddy Pig's office.

2 Peppa and _____ were in Daddy Pig's car.

3 "This is Mrs Cat," said

_____ .

4 "What do you do at your office?" asked _____ .

**4** **Choose the correct answers.**

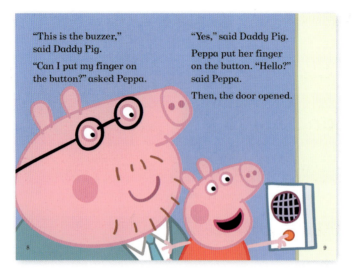

"This is the buzzer," said Daddy Pig.

"Can I put my finger on the button?" asked Peppa.

"Yes," said Daddy Pig.

Peppa put her finger on the button. "Hello?" said Peppa.

Then, the door opened.

**1** "This is the **computer,"** / **buzzer,"** said Daddy Pig.

**2** "Can I put my finger on the **door?"** / **button?"**

**3** **"Yes,"** / **"No,"** said Daddy Pig.

**4** Peppa put her **finger** / **hand** on the button.

**5** Then the **buzzer** / **door** opened.

**5** **Complete the sentences.**
   **Write a—d.**

1 "This is the elevator,"                          b

2 "Can I put my                                    ............

3 "No, George can put                              ............

4 George put his finger                            ............

---

**a** his finger on it," said Daddy Pig.

**b** said Daddy Pig.

**c** finger on the button?" asked Peppa.

**d** on the elevator button.

---

**6** **Look at the letters.**
**Write the words.** 🖊 ✏

1 ( D d d y a )

D a d d y Pig

2 ( t e l o e v r a )

............ ............ ............ ............ ............ ............ ............ ............

3 ( f f i o c e )

............ ............ ............ ............ ............ ............

4 ( z u b z r e )

............ ............ ............ ............ ............ ............

5 ( t a C )

Mrs ............ ............ ............

## 7 Who said this?

Daddy Pig    Peppa

**1** "This is the elevator," said
Daddy Pig .

**2** "Can I put my finger on the button?"
asked ........................................... .

**3** "No, George can put his finger on it,"
said ........................................... .

**4** "This is Mrs Cat," said
........................................... .

**5** "Hello, Mrs Cat," said
........................................... .

**8** **Ask and answer questions about the picture with a friend.**

**1**
> *Who is sitting at her desk?*

> *Mrs Cat is sitting at her desk.*

**2** What is on her desk?

**3** Who is in her office?

**4** Who is next to Peppa?

**9** **Look and read. Choose the correct words and write them on the lines.** 📖 ✏️ ⭐

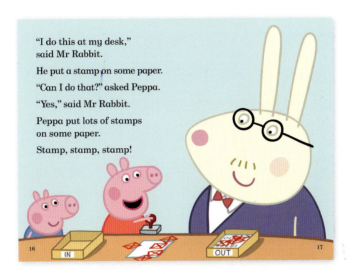

> "I do this at my desk," said Mr Rabbit.
>
> He put a stamp on some paper.
>
> "Can I do that?" asked Peppa.
>
> "Yes," said Mr Rabbit.
>
> Peppa put lots of stamps on some paper.
>
> Stamp, stamp, stamp!

| desk | Rabbit | Peppa | stamp |

**1** "I do this at my ........ *desk* ........," said Mr Rabbit.

**2** He put a ................ on some paper.

**3** "Can I do that?" asked ................ .

**4** "Yes," said Mr ................ .

**10** **Look and read. Match the two parts of the sentences.**

**1** Mrs Cat has got a

**2** Mrs Cat drew a

**3** "Can I do that?"

**4** Peppa is in front of

**5** George is in front of

**a** picture on her computer.

**b** Peppa.

**c** Daddy Pig.

**d** computer and a printer on her desk.

**e** asked Peppa.

**11** **Circle the correct pictures.**

**1** George drew this.

 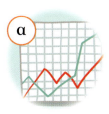

**2** George put his finger on this.

 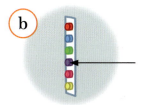

**3** Peppa and George like these.

 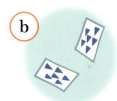

**4** This is not paper.

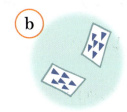

**12** Write *print*, *printer*, or *printed*.

**1** Print, _____print_____, print!

**2** Peppa and George _____
with Mrs Cat's printer.

**3** They liked Mrs Cat's computer and
_____.

**4** The printer could _____
lots of pictures.

## 13 Look, match, and write the words.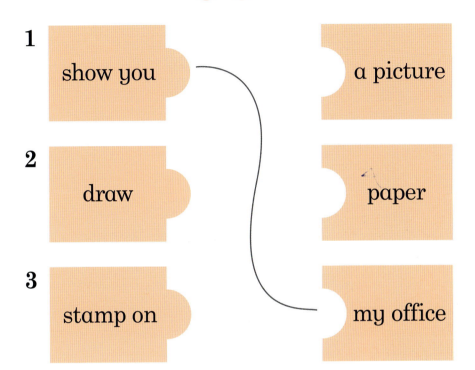

1 show you          a picture

2 draw              paper

3 stamp on          my office

1 ....show you my office....

2 ..............................

3 ..............................

43

**14** **Read the text. Choose the correct words and write them next to 1—5.**

elevator    pens    computer
printer    stamp

Peppa and George went up in the

1 __elevator__. Mrs Cat had a

computer and a 2 _____

on her desk. Mr Rabbit had some

paper and a 3 _____.

Peppa and George made a picture on

Mrs Cat's 4 _____.

Daddy Pig did not have a computer.

He had paper and 5 _____.

**15** Work with a friend. You are George. Your friend is Peppa. Ask and answer questions. 💬 ❓

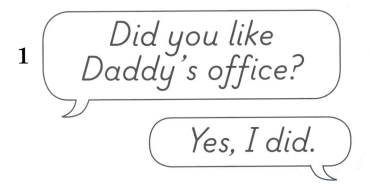

**1** Did you like Daddy's office?

Yes, I did.

**2** Whose job did you like? Why? / Why not?

**3** What did you do today?

**16** **Read the questions. Write the answers.** 📖 ✏️

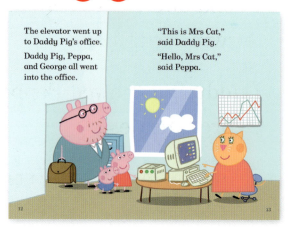

The elevator went up to Daddy Pig's office.

Daddy Pig, Peppa, and George all went into the office.

"This is Mrs Cat," said Daddy Pig.

"Hello, Mrs Cat," said Peppa.

**1** Did the elevator go up or down to Daddy Pig's office?

The elevator went up to Daddy Pig's office.

**2** Who did Peppa and George see in the office?

Peppa and George saw _____

_____.

**3** Who said, "This is Mrs Cat"?

_____.